Grumpy Ol

written by Jay Dale

illustrated by Jacqueline East

Grumpy Old Bear
was in the forest.
He was sitting by a tree.

"Who are you?"
said Grumpy Old Bear.

"I am Little Squirrel,"
said Little Squirrel.
"I am new here."

3

"Then go away,"
said Grumpy Old Bear.
"Go back to your forest!
This is **my** forest."

4

Little Squirrel ran back
to her forest.

Grumpy Old Bear

was down by the pond.

He was sitting by the water.

6

"Who are you?"
said Grumpy Old Bear.

"I am Brown Duck,"
said Brown Duck.
"I am new here."

7

"Then go away,"
said Grumpy Old Bear.
"Go back to your pond!
This is **my** pond."

8

Brown Duck went back
to his pond.

Grumpy Old Bear
was sitting by his cave.

10

"Who are you?"
said Grumpy Old Bear.

"I am Black Bat,"
said Black Bat.
"I am new here."

11

"Then go away,"
said Grumpy Old Bear.
"Go back to your cave!
This is **my** cave."

12

Black Bat went back
to her cave.

Grumpy Old Bear got up.
"I will look for my friends,"
he said.

But they had all run away!